WERE WOLF!

Hide your children, lock your doors,
lest you be seen, nevermore.

The beast is skulking all around,
The werewolf comes when the sun goes down.

As the moon begins to rise,
the stars come out and fill the skies.

They listen quietly to the stillness of the night.

The crickets chirp
and frogs croak,
and through it all,
they hear a sound.

AWWOOOOO

A cry from somewhere deep into the woods.
"There!" Culania says, "that way Shalim!"

"Yes, let's run towards the monster." she laughs
"Remind me again how you defeated Night-Mare."

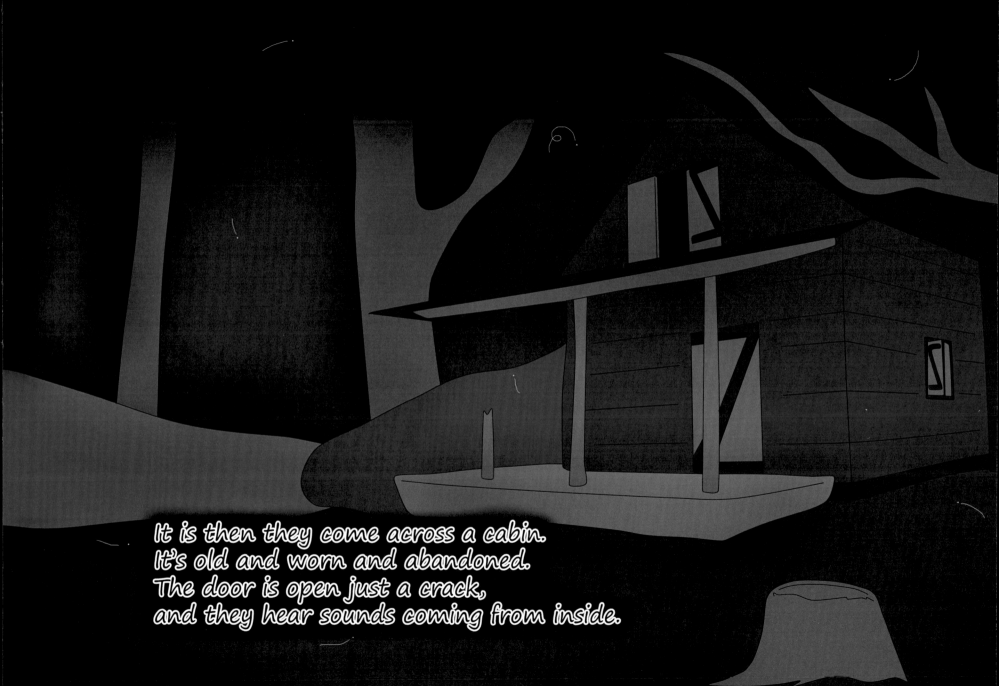

It is then they come across a cabin.
It's old and worn and abandoned.
The door is open just a crack,
and they hear sounds coming from inside.

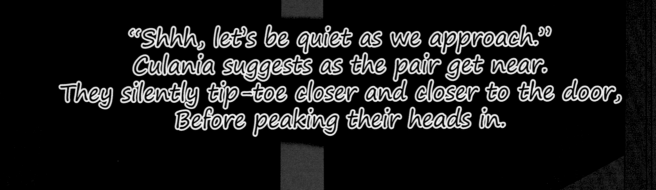

"Shhh, let's be quiet as we approach."
Culania suggests as the pair get near.
They silently tip-toe closer and closer to the door,
Before peaking their heads in.

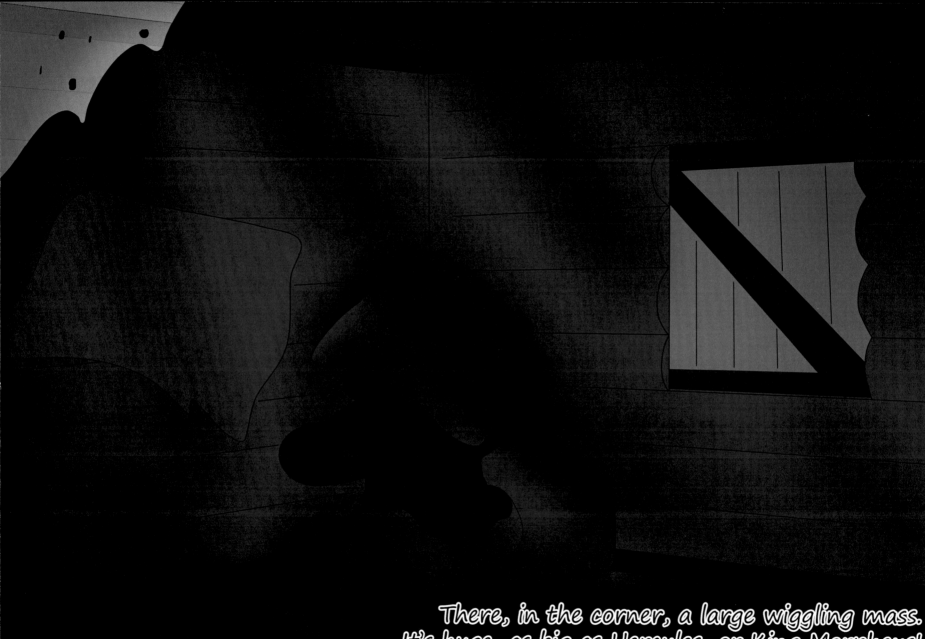

There, in the corner, a large wiggling mass.
It's huge, as big as Hercules, or King Morpheus!
It's looking away from them. "Hello?" Culania weakly asks.

Quickly it turns and spots them,
Its large dark eyes staring down at them,
It lunges backward deeper into the corner.
"No! No hurt me!" it cries.

This caught both of them off guard,
and they jump in fright!
"We're not going to hurt you,"
Shalim quickly says.

It breathes heavily,
"Promise?"

"I promise!"
Culania tells it.

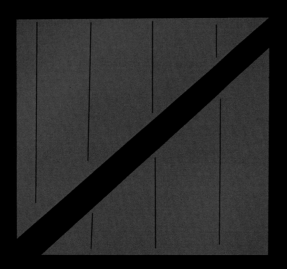

The werewolf comes a bit closer,
"Who... are... you...?" she asks.

"I'm Prince Culania, and this is Shalim.
We've been looking for you."

"People are mad that you broke some things."

"Sorry..." it huffs.
"Don't know. Own strength."
She grabs her tail in her paws.
"Clumsy."

"What about the howling?" Shalim asks.

"Father, wait! She's not bad!" Culania pleads.
"She's my friend! She never meant to hurt anyone!"

"Please, listen to him!" Shalim begs.

"I won't let you hurt her Father,
it isn't right!"

Morpheus looks at his son, the family friend,
And the whimpering werewolf behind them.
He lowers his sword and laughs.
"Looks like you have a story for me, son."

And so she became the castle's new maid.
She's clumsy but gets better every day.
And at night she still finds time to play
With Culania and Shalim and other friends that come their way.

CPSIA information can be obtained
at www.ICGtesting.com
Printed in the USA
LVRC101622170622
721365LV00003B/14